Ro... Long
Gets It Wrong

David O'Doherty

Illustrated by David Roberts

Mammoth

For my grandparents
D. O'D.

For Nichola and Mark
D.R.

First published in Great Britain in 2000
by Mammoth, an imprint of Egmont Children's Books Limited,
a division of Egmont Holding Limited
239 Kensington High Street, London W8 6SA

Text copyright © 2000 David O'Doherty
Illustrations copyright © 2000 David Roberts

The moral rights of the author and illustrator have been asserted.

ISBN 0 7497 4450 2

10 9 8 7 6 5 4 3

A CIP catalogue record for this book
is available from the British Library

Printed in Reading, Berkshire
by Cox & Wyman Ltd.

Contents

~

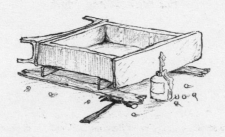

1. The fastest bookshelf in the world

It was a cold Friday afternoon and Ronan Long was outside wrapped up in his warm jacket and gloves. He was digging for dinosaur fossils in the dinosaur pit by his inventing shed. Ronan hadn't ever found a dinosaur fossil in the pit — not so far anyway — but he had found a few other things. They were all listed on a big chart that was hung inside the shed.

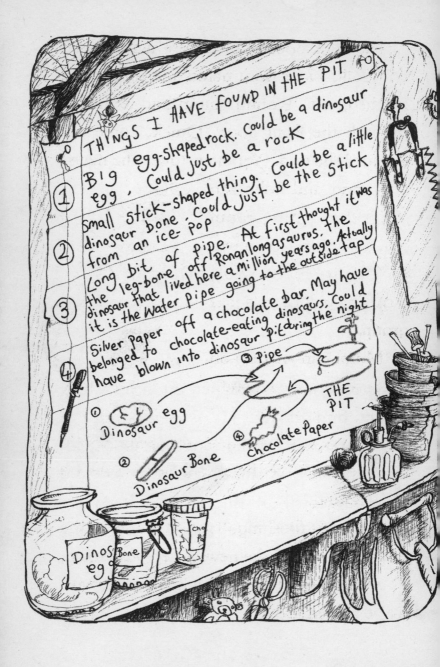

The back door of the house swung open and Sally Little from across the road stuck her head out. Ronan's mum had let her in through the front door. 'Quick, come on, Ronan,' she said. 'You have to see the news.'

Ronan and Sally ran into the sitting-room where Ronan's mum was practising her double bass. She played in a jazz group.

'Mum, can we turn on the news for one second?' asked Ronan.

Ronan's mum was quite shocked. He had never asked to see the news before. 'Sure, go on,' she said.

It was just finishing. 'Now it's time for the weather forecast,' the newscaster was saying.

'Aww,' said Ronan, 'whatever it was, we've missed it.'

'No,' said Sally. 'This is the bit you have to see.'

The whole weather map was covered in big white snow clouds.

'Heavy snowfalls are expected tonight in the east and the south and the north and west,' the weatherman said.

Ronan bounced up and cheered. It was the greatest news ever. Finally he would get to see some real snow. It hadn't snowed on Shackleton Road since before he was born.

'Quick,' he said to Sally. 'Let's build a toboggan.'

'There's some wood in the skip outside Complainey Delaney's,' said Sally. 'We can use that.'

'Now hang on a second,' Ronan's mum interrupted. 'I don't want anyone taking anything from anywhere without asking. That's stealing, and you know how easy it is to annoy Mr Delaney.'

Mr Delaney lived next door to Sally and was the world's complainiest man. He liked giving out to people more than Ronan Long liked inventing.

'But it wouldn't be stealing,' Ronan tried to argue. 'It would just be . . . recycling.'

His mum gave him one of her looks.

'Don't worry,' said Sally, who always knew the right thing to say to grown-ups. 'We'll go over and ask if we can have some of his wood.'

Sally and Ronan didn't even have to ring his doorbell to get their answer. An upstairs window slid open as they came towards his gate.

'Get away from my skip. I've caught you red-handed about to rob my wood . . . blah, blah . . . You have no respect for senior

5

citizens . . . blah, blah . . .' This was Mr Delaney at his complainey best.

Sally tried to be her most polite. 'Good afternoon, Mr Delaney. We were just going to ask you if we could please have a tiny bit of the old wood you are throwing out . . . If that would be OK . . . Please.'

'Don't pretend you weren't about to steal it,' Complainey went on. 'Now get lost and keep your thieving hands away from my property.' The window slammed shut.

6

Sally and Ronan walked back across the road.

'Trust Complainey to guard his rubbish,' muttered Ronan.

Just then, Molly Rice came cycling along the path. It was her dad's birthday in a few days and she was off to buy a present from her and her brother Ben.

'What are you going to get?' Sally inquired.

'I don't know. Maybe something to do with gardening, he likes that. Ben and I don't have much money though.'

'Did you hear about the snow?' asked Ronan.

Molly said she had. She had also heard Complainey Delaney shouting from his window. Sally explained about the toboggan and the wood.

'There's an old wooden bookshelf in the lane behind our house,' Molly said. 'You might be able to do something with that.'

Ten minutes later the bookshelf was in Ronan Long's back garden. Ten minutes after that it wasn't a bookshelf any more. Sally and Ronan had taken out the shelves and glued strips of wood, to act as skis, to the bottom. Now it was a toboggan big

enough for two. The only thing left to do was wait for the snow.

All night Ronan tried to imagine what Shackleton Road would look like in the morning. The white roofs on the houses, the white hats on the cars, the white front gardens, and then Shackleton Park covered in snow. Shackleton Park with its perfect hill for tobogganing.

Ronan was almost sure he could smell the snow when he woke up next morning.

8

Slowly he made his way over to the window, shut his eyes, slid the curtains open and peered outside. It looked . . . exactly the same as it normally did. Not a single flake of snow had fallen. In fact it was a bright and sunny morning. Ronan couldn't believe it. He ran downstairs to his mum.

'What happened to my snow?'

'The weather must have changed during the night. This looks like the first day of spring.'

'But . . . but what about the weather forecast?'

'They don't always get it right.'

Ronan unhappily chewed his way through breakfast. He felt like running outside and yelling up at the sky for not snowing. Then the doorbell rang.

It was Sally, and she had a new plan. Sally was great at thinking up new plans.

'If we just attach some wheels to the bottom of the toboggan then we don't need snow. It will roll down the hill in the park.'

Ronan suddenly cheered up. 'We can take the little wheels off the old bed in our back garden.' The old bed had been sitting outside the Long's kitchen window for years waiting to be thrown out.

'Perfect,' said Sally.

Ronan got dressed and they set to work. They unscrewed the legs of the bed and attached one to each corner of the toboggan. Soon it was ready for the park.

Molly and her brother Ben were helping their dad tidy the front garden when Ronan and Sally wheeled the new go-cart past.

'Come with us,' said Sally. 'You can help launch the fastest bookshelf in the world.'

'Did you get something for your dad at the shop?' Ronan asked as they pushed together up the hill in the park.

'No. Everything was too expensive,' said Molly.

'We have to think of something else soon,' Ben added. 'It's his birthday tomorrow so we haven't got very much time to think of something else or then we won't have anything and that will be bad.' Ben always used more words than he needed.

'Well, if you're stuck, we can give him a go on this,' suggested Ronan.

'I don't think he'd like that,' said Molly shaking her head.

When they reached the top of the hill, Sally and Ronan took their seats for the maiden voyage. Molly and Ben leaned on the back, ready for a big push-off.

'Ready,' said Molly, 'Steady . . .'

'Hold on,' Ronan butted in. 'Before the first ever run, I'd like to make a quick speech. Thanks to Sally my partner on the project, thanks to Molly for telling us about this old bookshelf, thanks to whoever used to own it, thanks to Complainey for not letting us have his wood, thanks to the weather for

12

not snowing, thanks to the weather forecaster for telling us that it would snow because then we wouldn't have had the idea to change the bookshelf into a toboggan in the first pla . . .'

'GO!' Sally shouted.

Molly and Ben started to push. The cart went forward a few centimetres but the weight of Ronan and Sally made it very difficult to move.  The little wheels dug deep into the grass on the hill. The harder they pushed, the deeper they dug.

'I'll get out and push,' said Sally jumping out. But it was no use. The bed wheels just weren't made for rolling down grassy hills.

Sally spoke. 'Ronan, I think what we have here is a won't-go-cart.'

'Maybe there's room for it in Complainey's skip,' said Ronan slowly and sadly, stepping out on to the grass.

'Maybe we could give it to our dad for his birthday,' joked Molly.

Suddenly Ronan perked up. 'That's it!' he exclaimed.

'I don't think our dad would really like it,' said Ben. 'Molly was only joking when she said that we could give it to our . . .'

'No,' interrupted Ronan. 'I know how we can make this into the perfect present for your dad.'

Back at Ronan's shed Molly and Ben were amazed when they saw what he was doing to the go-cart. He glued on two short handles, one sticking out from each side at the back, so it could be lifted up and pushed along.

Next morning their dad said it was his best ever birthday present. A wheelbarrow

14

for the garden, that had once been a
bookshelf, and a toboggan, and a go-cart.

2. Ronan gets a pet

'Would it be all right for Ronan to look after Florence for the day?' Sally Little asked Ronan Long's mum one morning. 'My dad and I are going to visit my granny, and we won't be back until late tonight.'

Florence was Sally's short black dog, with long ears that looked like extra legs when she ran towards you.

'Please, Mum, can I?' begged Ronan.

'Of course you can,' said Ronan's mum bending over to give Florence a pat.

16

Florence wagged her tail and smiled in a doggy sort of way.

Ronan was delighted. He had always wanted his own pet. His mum and dad said he could have one when he was old enough to look after it himself. Now was his chance to show them that he was.

Sally gave Ronan some food for Florence's dinner and her lead. 'Make sure she doesn't get into any trouble, won't you?' she whispered to Ronan when his mum had moved away.

'Don't worry, Sally,' chirped Ronan. 'I know what she's like.'

Everyone on Shackleton Road knew what Florence was like. She loved to woof and chase, and do all the things that dogs aren't supposed to do.

Ronan decided to take Florence to the park.

'Now, Florence, see this stick?' said Ronan holding one out. 'Well, when I throw it, you run after it and bring it back to me.'

Florence looked up as if she understood.

'Now, GO!' Ronan threw the stick as far as he could and Florence galloped after it. 'Good dog!' he shouted as she ran towards it . . .

But then straight past . . .

And SPLASH! into the pond where the ducks were swimming.

'FLORENCE!' Ronan shouted as the ducks flapped up into the sky. He reached the edge of the pond just as she was climbing out. 'Look at you.'

Florence was dripping wet and starting to shiver.

'Let's go home and get you dry.' He clipped her lead on and they set off.

Ronan found the biggest bath towel in the house and wrapped Florence up in it. She liked that. In no time she was dry and out charging around the back garden.

'What's that bath towel doing in here?' Ronan's mum asked when she came down to the kitchen.

'Ah, the bath towel, er . . .' Ronan didn't want to tell her what had really happened. It would look as though he wasn't able to look after a dog. 'I got caught in the rain on the way home from the park . . . and I didn't want to have wet hair and catch a cold-a-a-

ATISHOO.' The sneeze came just at the right time.

'I see,' said Ronan's mum. 'Are you feeling all right now?'

'Yes. I'm fine-a-a-ATISHOO . . . I'm just going out to see what Florence is doing.'

Ronan opened the back door and headed out. Ronan's mum stood staring out of the window, wondering why it didn't look as if it had been raining.

 Outside, Florence was woofing at things she didn't like. She didn't like the cat sitting on the wall, or the sound of Elvis the budgie next door, or her own reflection in the window of Ronan's inventing shed.

'Ssh, Florence.' Ronan didn't want her to wake his dad. He was asleep upstairs. He worked at nights, driving a taxi, and slept until dinner-time every day. 'Come on, let's go inside and watch the telly.'

20

Florence wasn't very interested in the television, even when Ronan found a cartoon with a dog in it. She was more interested in going off to explore the Longs' house.

'Ronan!' Ronan's mum called out a little while later. 'Why are all of your shoes in the hall?'

Ronan went out for a look. Sure enough, there they were, in a big pile.

'Ah . . . my shoes. Yes. I brought them all down to polish them.' It was the only thing he could think of.

'Did you?' said Ronan's mum.

'ATISHOO!' Ronan still hadn't stopped sneezing.

'But I thought you hated polishing your shoes?'

'I normally do but . . .' he stopped to think of what to say next. 'But I thought they could all do with a good polish.'

'Well, go ahead, then.'

'I will,' said Ronan.

Just then, Florence bounced down the stairs with one of his slippers in her mouth. Ronan's mum gave him a puzzled look.

'Good girl,' said Ronan. 'I asked her to bring it down.'

Ronan's mum started to walk away,

but stopped and turned back.
'Don't polish them in the hall.'

'No.'

'And, Ronan?'

'Yes.'

'Don't polish your slippers.'

Florence was well behaved for the rest of the afternoon. She sat on the floor in his shed while he worked on his latest invention:

a box with a lid to stop dogs stealing shoes. Then she sniffed around the kitchen while Ronan did all the shoe polishing he hadn't intended to do.

Soon it was time for dinner and Florence noisily guzzled hers on the floor while the

Long family ate at the table. Ronan didn't feel very well. His eyes were watering and he couldn't stop sneezing.

'Maybe we should go and see the doctor in the morning,' said Ronan's mum.

Ronan's dad was up now and he gave Ronan a big bowl of ice-cream for dessert. He said that ice-cream sometimes makes sick people feel better, but poor Ronan couldn't even finish his. He went upstairs for a lie down.

Ronan lay on his bed listening to the sound of the television downstairs. His mum and dad were watching a quiz.

'Complete this expression,' the host was saying, '"Raining cats and . . ."' It made Ronan think of Florence. Where was she? Suddenly a huge crashing sound came from the kitchen. Ronan sprang up and ran down the stairs to see what had happened. The bin was on the floor and there was rubbish everywhere. Ronan took one look at the mess and quickly began clearing it up. Just then, his mum and dad appeared at the kitchen door.

'What's going on here?' asked Ronan's dad.

'Oh, nothing,' said Ronan. 'I'm just checking the rubbish to see . . . to see if we cut all the tokens off the back of the breakfast cereal box.'

'I thought you were upstairs having a lie down,' said Ronan's mum.

'Ah, yes, I was,' said Ronan. 'But then I

started to think about, um, the free sports bag we can get if we collect all the . . .'

Florence appeared from under the table. Her head was hunched close to the ground, as if she knew she had done something wrong. There was ice-cream all over her ears and face.

'It looks to me like somebody knocked the bin over to get the end of your ice-cream,' Ronan's mum said.

Ronan couldn't lie any more. 'I didn't want you to think that I'm not old enough to look after-a-a-ATISHOO! a dog, but I'm sure that's what you think now.'

'Not at all,' said Ronan's dad. 'In fact we were just talking about how well you were doing. We all know that Florence isn't like most dogs . . . She's like, well, Florence.'

That cheered Ronan up. 'So, do you think we could ask at the pet shop about getting a pet? A dog, or a cat, or a-a-

ATISHOO . . . anything?'

'I think we'll visit the doctor first and find out what's wrong with you,' said Ronan's mum.

Ronan was fast asleep when Sally and her dad called to pick Florence up later that evening.

Next morning he felt much better. Still, his mum insisted they pay a visit to Dr Rice. It didn't take her very long to figure out what had been wrong with Ronan.

'I'm afraid you have a very strong allergic reaction to animals,' the doctor announced.

'What does that mean?' Ronan asked.

'Well, if you spend too much time around dogs or cats, or any animal with a thick coat of hair, your eyes will water, you'll start to sneeze and you won't feel well.'

'Oh no,' moaned Ronan.

'We were going to see about getting a pet today,'

Ronan's mum explained.

'Well, there are still plenty of pets you can get,' said Dr Rice. 'How about a fish?'

'No,' said Ronan. He always felt sorry for fish swimming around little bowls all day.

'A tortoise?'

Ronan shook his head. Tortoises slept for the whole winter.

'A budgie, then?'

'No. The Drums next door have one called Elvis, and his singing keeps them awake all night.'

'I have an idea,' said Ronan's mum.

They left the doctor's and drove straight to the garden centre.

'This is stupid,' said Ronan grumpily. 'They don't sell pets here.'

'Oh yes they do.'

His mum led him to the greenhouse

section. 'You are about to become the owner of the first ever pet cactus.'

Ronan wasn't sure about the idea until he saw all the different ones they had. Some were tall and skinny, others short and round, one looked as though it was from a cowboy movie.

'That's the one I want,' said Ronan, pointing at it. It was yellow and green with a red pot. Ronan's mum picked out a book as well: *How to look after your cactus*.

'Have you thought of a name for your pet?' she asked in the car on the way home.

'Yes I have,' said Ronan. 'I'm going to call him Spike.'

3. Ronan and Mark

'Begin the countdown to take-off!' Ronan Long called out from the other side of Shackleton Park.

'Countdown commencing,' Charlie Drum, Ronan's next door neighbour answered. Beside Charlie, his little brother Mark sat on Ronan's old blue BMX bike . . . Ronan's old blue BMX bike except with huge sweeping-brush-and-cardboard wings attached to its handlebars. It was the first ever test run of Ronan's latest invention, the Fly-Cycle – the bike that can fly. Mark Drum was the official tester. Ronan looked on with his notebook and pencil.

Charlie started the countdown. 'Five, four . . .'

Mark put his foot on the pedal, ready to ride off and upwards. He had his brother's old red skateboard helmet on his head and, on his back, a bag Ronan had given him with cheese sandwiches and a bottle of orange squash, in case he got hungry while he was in the sky.

'Three, two, ONE!' Charlie gave his brother a gentle push and watched as the Fly-Cycle moved off across the grass.

1. VERY HARD TO STEER was the first thing that Ronan noted down in his notebook. The bike was wobbling from side to side as it rolled towards him. It seemed to want to go to the left, towards the bushes and the flowerbeds.

'Don't go that way . . . come over here!' Ronan shouted. But shouting at Mark only made him panic. He was doing his best to steer away from the bushes but the weight of wings on the handlebars made it very hard.

2. *NEVER SHOUT AT THE TESTER* Ronan wrote in his notebook.

Ronan was sure that if Mark could just get up enough speed, the bike would take off into the air, like an aeroplane. Mark was beginning to go faster, but the bushes were getting much too close.

'STOP!' shouted Ronan.

Mark grabbed the brakes . . . but nothing happened. They weren't working.

3. *REMEMBER TO FIX BRAKES ON BI . . .* Ronan was just writing when he heard Mark cry out.

'HELP!'

The edge of the left-hand wing clipped a bush and the Fly-Cycle turned in a sharp

semicircle and flopped on to the ground.

Ronan and Charlie ran over to see how the pilot was. Mark didn't look too well. He lay on the ground holding his ankle.

'I'm really sorry, Mark,' said Ronan. 'I should have checked the brakes.'

'I think I'd better go home,' mumbled Mark, doing his best to hold in tears.

Ronan pulled off what was left of the wings, while Charlie helped his brother up on to one foot. Together they gently lifted Mark on to the saddle and wheeled him back to the front door of 26 Shackleton Road.

Charlie and Mark's mum took one look at the ankle and decided that she should take Mark to Casualty.

Ronan spent most of the evening staring out of the window, hoping to see the Drums' blue car come back from the hospital. He wanted to apologise again for the accident. But, as usual, the hospital took ages. It was long after Ronan had gone to sleep that Mark finally hobbled out of the car on a pair of crutches and went to bed.

Ronan got up early the next morning and made a Sorry-and-Get-Well-Soon card for Mark. It had a picture of Mark in the sky, fly-cycling past an aeroplane. Inside was written, 'Sorry about the crash and I hope you will be flying around again soon.'

Charlie answered the door when Ronan called round with the card.

'Well, he didn't break anything, and that's good news,' explained Charlie. 'He sprained his ankle. The bad news is that he has to rest it. The doctor says he can't walk around for a week.'

'Where is he now?' asked Ronan. 'I've made something for him.'

'In there.' Charlie pointed towards the sitting-room. 'But look out, he's in a really bad mood.'

'Don't worry, I'll cheer him up,' said Ronan, pushing the door open.

Mark was lying on the sofa staring at the television. His sore ankle was wrapped in a thick white bandage.

'Hey, Mark, I'm really sorry about what happened yesterday. In future I'll test my own inventions.'

Mark didn't say anything.

'How does it feel today?'

Still Mark didn't say anything.

'I bet it's very sore. If there's anything I can do to help, just ask.'

Mark's eyes were fixed on the television screen and his mouth was shut tight.

'Look,' said Ronan reaching into his back

pocket. 'I made you a card . . .'

It was a bit squished, but Ronan knew Mark wouldn't mind – not normally anyway. Ronan held it out but Mark wouldn't even lift a hand to take it. He just kept staring.

'I'll leave it up here,' said Ronan nervously, putting the card on the mantelpiece.

'No,' snarled Mark.

'How about over here on the table?'

'Don't bother,' Mark snapped. 'Take your stupid card and put it in a big bin somewhere with all of your stupid inventions that never work and are useless.'

Now Ronan didn't know what to say.

Mark went on, 'It's all your fault that I have to lie here for ages and ages being bored with a sore ankle. I can't even get up to change the channels on the stupid telly. I hope I never see you again.'

Ronan slowly edged towards the door, muttered another, 'Sorry,' and rushed out of the Drums' house and back into his own.

'I didn't know the brakes on the BMX didn't work,' Ronan whispered to Spike his pet cactus. He had lifted Spike's pot down from the windowsill and was lying beside him on the floor of his bedroom. 'It was just an accident. It wasn't really anybody's fault.'

Ronan looked around his room. As usual there were a few inventions and bits of inventions he was working on scattered about the place. 'They don't all deserve to go into a big bin, do they?' he asked his pet.

Ronan would have been the first to admit that not all of his inventions were perfect. And maybe some, like the roller blades for dogs, or the bookmark made of ice, for example, weren't such great ideas. But then there were the really good ones. Over on his

desk were the plans for the Ronan Long Mobile Phone, a mobile phone that was so mobile you didn't even have to carry it around.

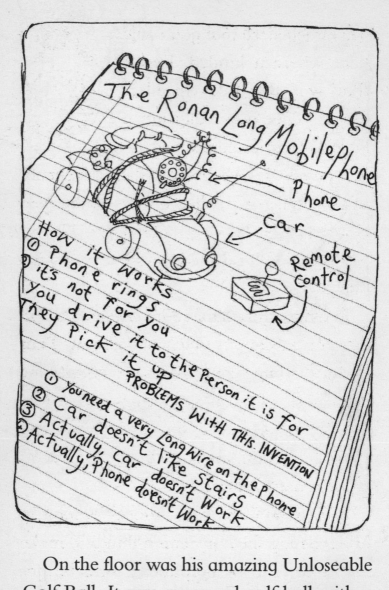

On the floor was his amazing Unloseable Golf Ball. It was a normal golf ball with a bell attached, so that you could hear where it landed. Beside that was the Bike-Speeder-Upper. That was really just a balloon with a clothes peg on it. You attached the balloon to the back carrier of your bike and pulled off the clothes peg when you needed to go a bit faster. The air from the balloon would blow your bike along.

Looking around the room cheered Ronan up. 'My inventions aren't all rubbish. That was just Mark being miserable because he has a sore ankle.' It gave him an idea too. 'Maybe I can cheer him up by inventing some useful things to help him while his ankle is getting better.'

So Ronan Long spent that afternoon in his inventing shed, inventing things to make life easier for his neighbour until he got better. After dinner that evening Ronan called in next door to show Mark what he had made.

'Not you again,' said Mark as Ronan opened the sitting-room door, dragging a black bin bag of inventions behind him.

'Yes, it's me. And I've brought a few things for you.'

'I hope they're not your inventions,' said Mark.

'They are, but really good ones. The first I call the Underneath-Your-Bandage-Scratcher,' Ronan said, pulling a school ruler with a bit of bendy wire attached to one end from the sack. 'It's so you can get to scratch itchy bits right in under your bandage.'

Mark looked quite impressed. 'What else have you got there?'

'This,' said Ronan, pulling a small black fishing reel from the bag. 'It's an automatic door opener. You can open the sitting-room door without even getting up.'

'It looks like a fishing reel to me,' said Mark.

'But look what it does,' said Ronan, tying one end of the fishing line to the handle of the door. 'Now, wind it in.'

From his place on the sofa, Mark started to wind and the sitting-room door swung open.

'Wow,' said Mark, 'that's good.'

'Next, here is something you'll really like.' Ronan pulled out the handle of one of the sweeping brushes that had been a wing on the Fly-Cycle. 'It's a remote control for your telly.'

The Drums had an old television set with buttons you had to get up and press. But with Ronan's remote control, you could poke them with the end of the brush while lying on the sofa.

'Now that's amazing!' said Mark.

'Wait till you see the last thing.' Ronan reached deep into the sack and pulled out a box with *Skrabble with a K* written on it in big letters.

'What is it?' asked Mark.

'It's a word game with a board and a bag of letters. You have to pick out letters and make words with them. But the words you make all have to be spelled a little bit wrong.'

'So you could spell "ankle" a–n–c–l–e . . .

or, a–n–k–a–l?' said Mark.

'That's exactly it,' said Ronan.

It sounded like a great game to Mark. 'Thanks for inventing all of this stuff for me,' he said. 'And I'm sorry about being mean and grumpy earlier.'

'I don't mind,' said Ronan. 'We're all in bad form sometimes. Now, call Charlie and let's see if we can come up with some bad spellings, OK?'

'Don't you mean OQ?' said Mark laughing.

4. Ronan Long gets it wrong

'I have some very serious news for you all,' said Ronan Long to Sally, Charlie, Molly and Ben. He had asked them to meet him in the tree-house in Sally Little's back garden, but hadn't told them why yet.

'Let me guess,' said Molly. 'You've finally dug up a dinosaur in your pit . . .'

'Or pirate treasure, or oil, or gold,' added Ben.

'No,' Ronan snapped. 'I said this is serious.'

46

'Bodies, then,' said Charlie smiling. 'You've dug up dead bodies.'

'Will you stop joking,' said Ronan stamping his foot on the floor and making the whole tree shake. 'It's much worse than that . . .'

Just then there was a noise from outside: the creak of a window opening next door. Everyone knew what that sound meant. Uh-oh. It was Complainey Delaney sticking his head out to complain about something.

'You young people up in that stupid tree-house,' he began, 'shouting and banging on the floor just to torment me . . . blah, blah . . . a complete lack of respect for senior citizens . . . blah, blah.' As usual he went on and on.

Sally leaned out of the tree-house. 'Sorry, Mr Delaney, we'll try to keep it down. It's just that Ronan is about to tell us some really serious news.'

'I hope it's that he's going away and never coming back!' shouted Complainey meanly.

Suddenly Florence the dog appeared from behind a bush in Complainey's back garden. She was carrying a pair of his huge stripy underpants in her mouth. She must have jumped up and grabbed them off his washing-line.

'Drop my underpants!' Complainey shouted as everyone else started to laugh. Florence jumped back into Sally's garden and ran into her house with them.

'I'll be telling all of your parents about this!' roared Complainey as he slammed his window shut again.

'And I'm sure they'll all find it very funny,' said Sally, leaning back into the tree-house.

'Now, what was that news you had for us?' asked Molly.

Ronan made a sad face. 'Complainey must know about it.'

'Know about what?' said Charlie.

'About my bad news,' said Ronan.

'Well what is it?' asked Sally.

'It's really bad.'

'Hurry up, come on and say the thing because we don't know what it is, the thing you are talking about,' said Ben.

'Earlier on, I was sitting on the bed in our back garden, and I heard my mum and dad talking in the kitchen . . .' He stopped and made another sad face.

'Come on, come on, say it,' said Sally.

Ronan took a big deep breath. 'We're moving house first thing in the morning. This is my last day ever living on Shackleton Road.'

'*What*?' everyone said at the same time. They couldn't believe it.

'But . . . but . . . where are you moving?' Ben wanted to know.

'I've no idea, but I bet it will be terrible and miles from here. All I heard them say was that we have to be packed up and ready to go first thing in the morning.'

Charlie was really shocked. 'But why? Why are you moving house? Why do your mum and dad want to move? Don't they like it here?'

'They do like it,' answered Ronan. 'I don't know why they want to go.'

'Well, why didn't you ask them when they told you about it?' Sally asked.

'Because they didn't tell me about it. I just heard them talking in the kitchen while I was in the back garden. When I went back inside, they had gone upstairs to pack up, so I came over here.'

For a second there was a glum silence in the tree-house but, during that same second, an idea popped into Sally Little's head. She had to think about how to say it, because she didn't want it to sound mean to Ronan.

'Ronan,' she began. 'Do you remember the time you saw the man in the fake beard and the fake bank-guard uniform stealing the money from the bank?'

'Yes?'

'And when you grabbed on to his leg to stop the robbery, it turned out that it wasn't a fake beard or a fake bank-guard uniform, because the man was a

real bank guard, and he was only moving the money into the bank-truck.'

Ben understood what Sally was getting at. 'Or remember the time you saw a huge flying dinosaur flying around the park, and you called the police to tell them that you had seen a huge flying dinosaur flying around the park, and they had to come and shoot it down or it would start flying around eating people, and when they came they found it was just a kite in the shape of a dinosaur that a little girl was flying?'

53

'Yes, I remember that too. What are you trying to say?'

Sally and Ben looked at each other. 'Just that things aren't always how they first seem . . .' Sally started to explain.

Molly knew what she meant and finished the sentence for her. 'And, sometimes, things that seem really bad at first aren't actually that bad when you find out the full story.'

'But how can this possibly not be bad?' Ronan wanted to know. 'It *is* the full story. I heard them talking about it. It's the worst news in the world.'

'Well, let's just make sure that it is before we all get sad about it,' said Sally. 'Let's go over and talk to your mum and dad.'

'All right, but it won't do any good.'

So Sally, Charlie, Molly, Ben and Ronan climbed out of the tree, and went across the road to ask Ronan's mum and dad a very big question.

Ronan's dad was sitting in his dressing-gown, listening to his mum practise her double bass, when everyone marched into the sitting-room in a line. At the back was Ronan. He still looked sad.

Ronan's mum noticed this. 'Why on earth are you looking so sad, Ronan? All of your friends are here.'

Ben started to explain. 'Well, see, Ronan is sad because he heard you say something earlier on today, and we are all here just to see if the thing he heard was a true thing, or

if it was just a thing that he didn't quite hear right, just before we get sad, even though Ronan is sure that the thing he heard is the right thing, and we should all be sad.'

Sometimes it was hard to understand what Ben was saying, and Ronan's dad was a bit confused. His mum understood though.

'Well, what did he hear earlier on?' she asked.

Sally told her. 'Ronan thought he heard you say that you are going; leaving Shackleton Road . . . tomorrow morning.'

Ronan's mum and dad looked at each other.

'You aren't . . . are you?' said Charlie.

'Well . . .' Ronan's mum began.

'We were going to tell you later on tonight,' his dad chipped in. 'But I suppose you were bound to find out before then.'

'Oh no,' said Molly.

'It was going to be a surprise, but now you know,' Ronan's mum said. 'We're leaving at nine o'clock tomorrow morning.'

'Some surprise,' said Ronan, shaking his head and staring down at the floor.

The others let out a big sad sigh. They couldn't believe it.

'So you were right, Ronan,' said Sally. 'Sorry for not believing you. Oh dear. This is a terrible thing.'

'Really bad,' said Charlie.

'No more Ronan.' Molly was sad now, too.

'But I don't understand why you didn't tell me,' said Ronan.

'Well,' his mum started to explain, 'it's just that the last time we went away, you insisted on bringing all of your inventions . . .'

'And there was no room in the car for anything else,' added his dad.

'Wait a second here,' said Sally. 'What do you mean "the last time you went away"? Ronan has lived here on Shackleton Road all his life.'

'I mean on holidays, the last time we went on holidays,' answered Ronan's mum. 'We're going on holiday tomorrow. You can bring Spike, if that's what's making you sad, Ronan.'

Suddenly all of Ronan's friends realised what was going on. They looked over at Ronan. A wide smile broke out across his face and he threw his arms into the air, like he had just scored a fantastic goal.

'Hang on,' said Ronan's dad. 'You didn't think we were . . .'

Ronan was too happy to listen. 'HOORAY!' he was saying as he bounced around the room. 'I got it wrong! I got it wrong!'

Ronan Long got it wrong.

If you enjoyed this
<u>MAMMOTH STORYBOOK</u>
look out for

Blair the Winner Theresa Breslin
Blair Makes a Splash Theresa Breslin
Grandmother Georgia's Hats Franzeska Ewart
Tyler and the Talk Stalk Annie Dalton
Dozy Rosy Annie Dalton
Jam Jar Genie Annie Dalton
Family Stuff Andrew Matthews
Fierce Milly Marilyn McLaughlin